Disney · PIXAR

INSIDE OUT

ANGER

by **Brittany Candau**
illustrated by **Jerrod Maruyama**

Disney PRESS
Los Angeles · New York

Hey! What are

YOU

looking at?!

Fine!
I'll introduce myself.
I'm
Anger.

You aren’t going to get all

touchy-feely now,

are you?

I hate it when people say weird things, like “Don’t have a cow!”

WHY WOULD I HAVE A COW?!

What does that even mean?!

“Don’t lose your temper!” they say.

Well, don't worry—I haven't lost it. IT'S RIGHT HERE!

I like to honk my way through the traffic jams of life.

And I make sure we

GET OUR HEAD IN THE GAME!

#1
#1

I've perfected the art of

stom

and glaring. Just in case anyone tries to put us in time-out.

ping

Time-out? Yeah, I don't

THI

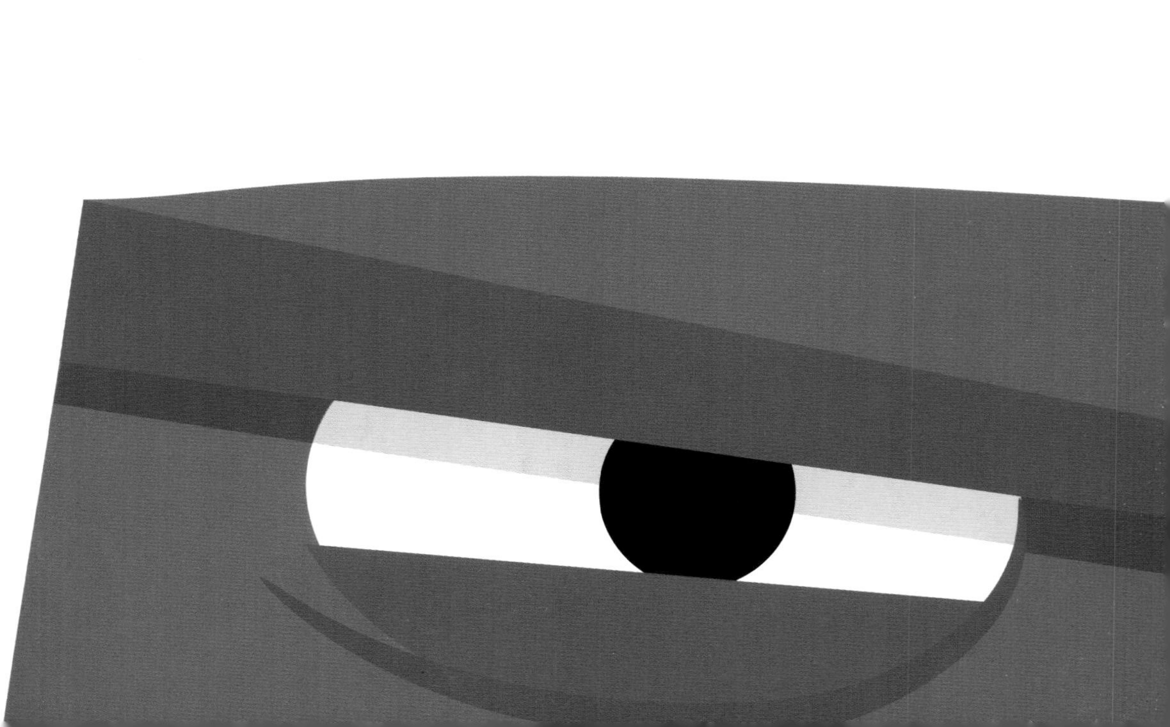

NK so!

But if there's one thing that burns me up . . .

more than
sunsets . . .

more than
scented
candles . . .

IT'S PUTTING

VEGETABLES

WHERE THEY DON'T BELONG!

BROCCOLI

ON PIZZA—YOU THINK I WOULDN'T NOTICE??!!

Ew. That is not food.